LITTLE FROG'S SONG

by Alice Schertle

pictures by
Leonard Everett Fisher

HarperCollins*Publishers*

For Chad and Jo Anne
—A.S.

Little Frog's Song
Text copyright © 1992 by Alice Schertle
Illustrations copyright © 1992 by Leonard Everett Fisher
Printed in the U.S.A. All rights reserved.
1 2 3 4 5 6 7 8 9 10
First Edition

Library of Congress Cataloging-in-Publication Data
Schertle, Alice.
    Little frog's song / by Alice Schertle ; pictures by Leonard
Everett Fisher.
      p.   cm.
    Summary: A little frog is washed away from his pond during a
storm.
    ISBN 0-06-020059-6. — ISBN 0-06-020060-X (lib. bdg.)
    [1. Frogs—Fiction. 2. Home—Fiction.] I. Fisher, Leonard
Everett, ill. Il. Title.
PZ7.S3442Li 1992   91-10405
[E]—dc20   CIP
                                                      AC

LITTLE FROG'S SONG

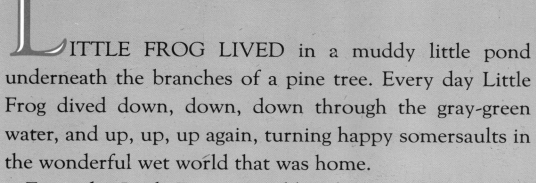

LITTLE FROG LIVED in a muddy little pond underneath the branches of a pine tree. Every day Little Frog dived down, down, down through the gray-green water, and up, up, up again, turning happy somersaults in the wonderful wet world that was home.

Every day Little Frog sunned his slippery body on a lily pad and watched the wind whisper through the water reeds.

Every evening, Little Frog watched the soft black night quietly cover the pond. He watched the silver moon roll up from behind a hill and slide through the branches of the pine tree.

Then, in the soft black darkness, Little Frog would sing. He sang of moon and mud and gray-green water. He sang of pond and pine and water reeds bending to the breeze.

One day, while Little Frog was busy napping on a lily pad, it began to rain. It rained and rained until the little pond was filled right up to the top. Little Frog didn't notice, because he was sound asleep.

It rained and rained until the pond overflowed, and the lily pad was washed away in a rainwater river. Little Frog still didn't notice, because he was sound asleep.

The rainwater river carried the lily pad with Little Frog on top past the pine, and around a rock, and across a road, and under a fence.

Finally the rain stopped, and the rainwater river stopped, and the lily pad stopped, and Little Frog stopped with it.

When Little Frog woke up, he looked all around. Where were the water reeds? Where was the pine? Where was the gray-green water? Where was the POND?

Little Frog made three big hops this way. *Hop! Hop! Hop!* There was no pond.

He made three big hops that way. *Hop! Hop! Hop!* Still there was no pond.

Hop! Hop! Hop! Hop! Hop! Hop! Hop! No matter which way he hopped, no matter where he looked, there was no pond. Little Frog had lost his home.

"Ba-a-a-a-a," said a voice, and there was a sheep.

Little Frog didn't know about sheep, but he knew enough not to take chances, so he hid under a leaf.

The sheep ate the leaf and stood blinking down at Little Frog.

Little Frog squeezed his eyes shut and waited to be eaten. When nothing happened, he said in his bravest voice, "I am Little Frog, and I have lost the pond. Can you tell me where my pond is?"

The sheep, who spoke a different language, didn't understand. But Little Frog could tell by her eyes that she was a gentle creature, so he followed her home to the meadow.

The sheep seemed happy to share her meadow with Little Frog. She showed him wild weeds and clumps of clover. She showed him meadow flowers humming with bees and a morning-glory vine all tangled up in a wire fence.

When evening came, the sheep settled down in a patch of clover, and Little Frog settled down beside her. He tried to sing, but the meadow had no music for a frog. Still, he saw that the same wind that whispered through the water reeds whispered through the meadow grasses, and he fell asleep dreaming of home.

The next morning Little Frog set out to find the pond. He hopped down a dusty road until he saw a dog trotting toward him. Little Frog didn't know about dogs, but he knew enough not to take chances, so he hid under a log.

When the dog drew near, his shiny black nose began to twitch. Soon he was sniffing and snuffing all around the log. He sniffed and snuffed until the log rolled over.

Little Frog squeezed his eyes shut and waited to be eaten. When nothing happened, he said in his bravest voice, "I am Little Frog, and I have lost the pond. Can you tell me where my pond is?"

The dog, who spoke a different language, didn't understand. But Little Frog could tell by his eyes that this was a gentle creature, so he followed him home to the doghouse.

The dog seemed happy to share his house with Little Frog. He showed Little Frog his water dish and his raggedy blanket and two bones and an old shoe that he chewed.

When evening came, the dog settled down on his raggedy blanket, and Little Frog settled down beside him. Little Frog tried to sing, but the doghouse had no music for a frog. Still, he saw that the same soft black night that quietly covered the pond quietly covered the doghouse, and he fell asleep dreaming of home.

In the morning, when a boy came out to feed the dog, Little Frog was sitting in the water dish. Little Frog didn't know about boys, but he knew enough not to take chances, so he hopped out of the water dish and hid behind it.

Down came the boy's hand and closed around Little Frog. Up the hand went and carried Little Frog very close to the boy's face.

Little Frog squeezed his eyes shut and waited to be eaten. When nothing happened, he said in his bravest voice, "I am Little Frog, and I have lost the pond. Can you tell me where my pond is?"

The boy, who spoke a different language, didn't understand. But he smiled, and Little Frog could tell by the boy's eyes that this was a gentle creature. So he wasn't afraid when the boy put him into his deep, dark pocket and carried him into a house.

The boy seemed happy to share his house with Little Frog. He showed Little Frog his room and his bed. He showed Little Frog all his toys. Then he put Little Frog in a glass bowl with a little water at the bottom and a flat rock in the middle.

When evening came, the boy settled down in his bed, and Little Frog settled down on the flat rock. Little Frog tried to sing, but the glass bowl had no music for a frog. Still, he saw that the same silver moon that shone over the pond shone through the open window, and he fell asleep dreaming of home.

In the morning, the boy took Little Frog out of the bowl and put him into his deep, dark pocket.

The boy walked and walked, and Little Frog rode along in the dark.

At last the boy took Little Frog out of his pocket and set him gently on the ground. After being in the dark pocket for so long, Little Frog had to blink his eyes in the bright sunlight. He blinked and blinked, and there was the pond! There was Little Frog's beautiful, muddy pond, ringed all around with water reeds.

Little Frog gave one mighty leap and splashed down in the middle of the gray-green water. Down, down, down he dived, and up, up, up again, turning happy somersaults in the wonderful wet world that was home.

When evening came, Little Frog watched the wind whisper through the water reeds. He watched the soft black night quietly cover his pond. He watched the silver moon roll up from behind a hill and slide through the branches of the pine tree.

And Little Frog began to sing.

He sang of moon and mud and gray-green water. "Home is home," sang Little Frog. "Home is home."

He sang of the wind and the reeds and the soft black night. "Home is home. Home is home."

In the meadow, the sleepy sheep raised her head.

In the doghouse, the sleepy dog stretched and sighed.

In his bed, the sleepy boy smiled and closed his eyes.
They heard Little Frog's song, and understood.
Home is home. Home is home.